Goldilocks & The Three Bears

© Published by Peter Haddock Limited
Bridlington, England
Printed in Italy

ph

NEVER-NEVER LAND STORIES

Goldilocks & The Three Bears

Illustrated by Stephanie Longfoot
Retold by Jenny Clayton

Once upon a time there was a little girl, called Goldilocks, who lived on the edge of the forest.

She was named Goldilocks because of the colour of her hair. It shone like gold in the sun.

Goldilocks had a naughty habit of running off to play and then getting lost. Her mother was always telling her to stay close to the house and not to play in the forest.

One day, as Goldilocks was sitting on her swing, she saw a little rabbit running into the forest.

"I wonder where he lives," thought Goldilocks, jumping off her swing and chasing after the rabbit.

On and on she ran, but Goldilocks could not keep up with the rabbit. Eventually she stopped running and realised she was lost.

Goldilocks was tired and also rather frightened.

"What if I can't find my way home? I wish I had listened to my mother."

She was just about to start crying when she noticed a small clearing in front of her.

Goldilocks went to investigate.

There in the clearing was a lovely, little cottage.

Goldilocks knocked on the door but there was no answer.

A window was open and Goldilocks peeped inside. It looked so inviting inside the cottage that she climbed through the window.

The three bears who lived in the cottage had only just gone out for a walk while their porridge, which Mother Bear had made, was cooling.

Goldilocks saw the three bowls of porridge and, as she was hungry, decided to try a little.

First she tried the big bowl, but it was too salty. Next she tried the medium-sized bowl, but it was too sweet. Finally she tried the little bowl and it tasted just right so she ate it all up.

Round the fireside were three chairs. Feeling tired, she tried to climb into the big chair, but it was much too high for her.

Next she tried the medium-sized chair but it was too hard.

She saw the little chair and tried to sit on it, but she was too big for it and it broke.

Goldilocks fell on to the floor.

In the corner of the room was a staircase which Goldilocks climbed.

At the top of the stairs was a bedroom with three beds in it.

Goldilocks was feeling tired so she decided to try the beds.

The big bed was so high that she could not even climb on to it.

The medium-sized bed was so soft, she disappeared into the mattress.

But there, in the corner, was a little bed. It was just the right size for Goldilocks.

Goldilocks was fast asleep when the bears returned from their walk.

Father Bear immediately noticed that someone had been inside the cottage.

"Somebody has been eating my porridge," growled Father Bear.

"Somebody has been eating my porridge," said Mother Bear.

"And somebody has eaten up all my porridge," cried Baby Bear.

Then Father Bear noticed his pipe lying on the floor. It had been on his chair.

"Who's been sitting on my chair?" roared Father Bear.

"Who's been sitting on my chair?" said Mother Bear in her gentle voice.

"And someone has been sitting on my chair and broken it all to pieces," cried the little bear and he burst into tears.

"Look, someone has left muddy footprints," growled Father Bear. "They go all the way up the stairs. Let's take a look."

The three bears went upstairs to investigate.

As soon as they went inside their bedroom, Father Bear roared in his loudest voice,

"Somebody has been lying on my bed."

Mother Bear said in her gentler voice,

"Somebody has been lying on my bed and they have made it untidy."

Baby Bear was staring at his bed.

"Somebody is in my bed," he squeaked in a frightened, little voice. "There. Fast asleep."

All three bears stared in astonishment at the pretty, little girl with the golden-coloured hair, sleeping in Baby Bear's bed.

The three bears wondered who she was.

"She's the one who ate all my porridge," cried Baby Bear. "She broke my chair," he wailed.

The little bear was making such a noise with his crying that Goldilocks woke up.

She got such a fright when she saw the three bears leaning over her that she jumped out of the bed, ran down the stairs and out through the front door.

Goldilocks never looked back. She ran as fast as she could through the woods until she reached the edge of the forest.

Her mother had been looking for her and was standing at the edge of the forest.

Goldilocks ran straight into her mother's arms and told her about the frightening experience she had had. She promised her mother that she would not wander off on her own ever again. Together, they walked home.

TITLES OF
NEVER-NEVER LAND STORIES

PINOCCHIO

CINDERELLA

PUSS IN BOOTS

SLEEPING BEAUTY

THE UGLY DUCKLING

PIED PIPER OF HAMELIN

BEAUTY AND THE BEAST

LITTLE RED RIDING HOOD

GOLDILOCKS AND THE THREE BEARS

SNOW WHITE AND THE SEVEN DWARVES